THE
AFRICAN UNION

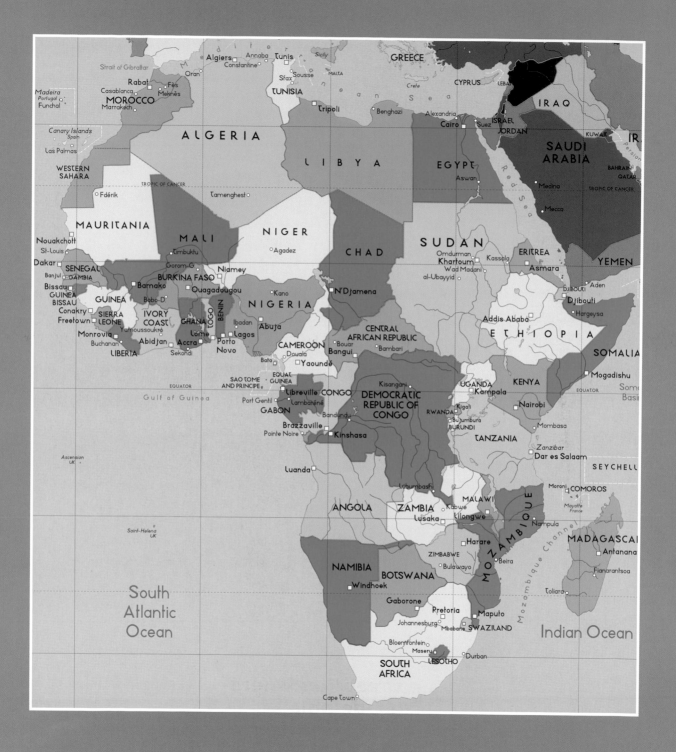

THE AFRICAN UNION

Russell Roberts

Mason Crest Publishers
Philadelphia

Produced by OTTN Publishing, Stockton, N.J.

Mason Crest Publishers
370 Reed Road
Broomall, PA 19008
www.masoncrest.com

First printing

1 3 5 7 9 8 6 4 2

Library of Congress Cataloging-in-Publication Data

  Roberts, Russell, 1953-
    The African Union / Russell Roberts.
        p. cm. — (Africa : continent in the balance)
    Includes bibliographical references and index.
    ISBN-13: 978-1-4222-0093-3
    ISBN-10: 1-4222-0093-0
  1. African Union—Juvenile literature. 2. Africa--Politics and government—1960—Juvenile literature.
  3. Africa—Economic conditions—1960—Juvenile literature. 4. Africa—Social conditions—
  1960—Juvenile literature. 5. Africa—History—1960—Juvenile literature. I. Title.
  DT30.5.R628 2007
  341.24'9—dc22

                                    2007010948

Table of Contents

Africa: Continent in the Balance
Robert I. Rotberg

Africa is the cradle of humankind, but for millennia it was off the familiar, beaten path of global commerce and discovery. Its many peoples therefore developed largely apart from the diffusion of modern knowledge and the spread of technological innovation until the 17th through 19th centuries. With the coming to Africa of the book, the wheel, the hoe, and the modern rifle and cannon, foreigners also brought the vastly destructive transatlantic slave trade, oppression, discrimination, and onerous colonial rule. Emerging from that crucible of European rule, Africans created nationalistic movements and then claimed their numerous national independences in the 1960s. The result is the world's largest continental assembly of new countries.

There are 53 members of the African Union, a regional political grouping, and 48 of those nations lie south of the Sahara. Fifteen of them, including mighty Ethiopia, are landlocked, making international trade and economic growth that much more arduous and expensive. Access to navigable rivers is limited, natural harbors are few, soils are poor and thin, several countries largely consist of miles and miles of sand, and tropical diseases have sapped the strength and productivity of innumerable millions. Being landlocked, having few resources (although countries along Africa's west coast have tapped into deep offshore petroleum and gas reservoirs), and being beset by malaria, tuberculosis, schistosomiasis, AIDS, and many other maladies has kept much of Africa poor for centuries.

Thirty-five of the world's 50 poorest countries are African. Hunger is common. So is rapid deforestation and desertification. Unemployment rates are often over 50 percent, for jobs are few—even in agriculture. Where Africa once was a land of small villages and a few large cities, with almost everyone

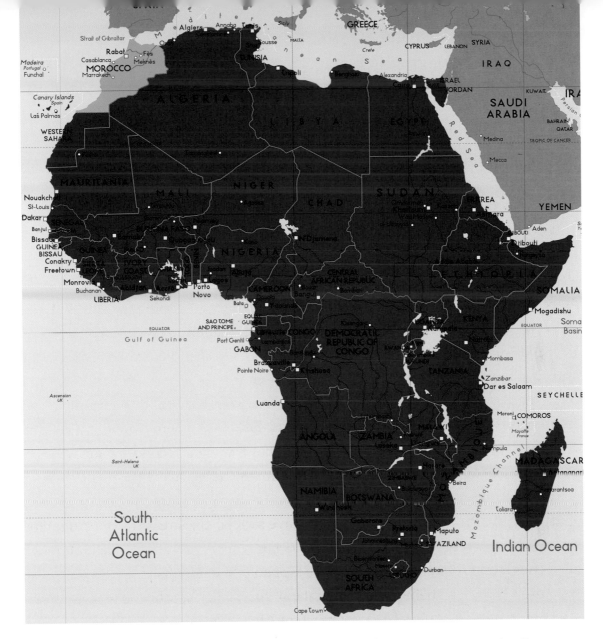

Fifty-three African countries are members of the African Union (AU), which was formed in 2002. Morocco refused to join the organization because the AU recognizes the Sahawri Arab Democratic Republic as the legitimate government of the Western Sahara territory, which Morocco also claims sovereignty over.

engaged in growing grain or root crops or grazing cattle, camels, sheep, and goats, today more than half of all the more than 900 million Africans, especially those who live south of the Sahara, reside in towns and cities. Traditional agriculture hardly pays, and a number of countries in Africa—particularly the smaller and more fragile ones—can no longer feed themselves.

There is not one Africa, for the continent is full of contradictions and variety. Of the 750 million people living south of the Sahara, at least 130 million live in Nigeria, 74 million in Ethiopia, 62 million in the Democratic Republic of the Congo, and 44 million in South Africa. By contrast, tiny Djibouti and Equatorial Guinea have fewer than 1 million people each, and prosperous Botswana and Namibia each are under 2.5 million in population.

Africa contains many natural resources and fascinating tourist attractions, from the lions and other wildlife of South Africa and the sub-Saharan savanna to the ancient pyramids of Egypt (Opposite).

Within some countries, even medium-sized ones like Zambia (11.5 million), there are a plethora of distinct ethnic groups speaking separate languages. Zambia, typical with its multitude of competing entities, has 70 such peoples, roughly broken down into four language and cultural zones. Three of those languages jostle with English for primacy.

Given the kaleidoscopic quality of African culture and deep-grained poverty, it is no wonder that Africa has developed economically and politically less rapidly than other regions. Since independence from colonial rule, weak governance has also plagued Africa and contributed significantly to the widespread poverty of its peoples. Only Botswana and offshore Mauritius have been governed democratically without interruption since independence. Both are among Africa's wealthiest countries, too, thanks to the steady application of good governance.

Aside from those two nations, and South Africa, Africa has been a continent of coups since 1960, with massive and oil-rich Nigeria suffering incessant periods of harsh, corrupt, autocratic military rule. Nearly every other country on or around the continent, small and large, has been plagued by similar bouts of instability and dictatorial rule. In the 1970s and 1980s Idi Amin ruled Uganda capriciously and Jean-Bedel Bokassa proclaimed himself emperor of the Central African Republic. Macias Nguema of Equatorial Guinea was another in that same mold. More recently Daniel arap Moi held Kenya in thrall and Robert Mugabe has imposed himself on once-prosperous Zimbabwe. In both of those cases, as in the case of the late Gnassingbe Eyadema in Togo and Mobutu Sese Seko in Congo, these presidents stole wildly and drove entire peoples and their nations into penury. Corruption is common in Africa, and so are weak rule-of-law frameworks, misplaced development, high expenditures on soldiers and low expenditures on health and education, and a widespread (but not universal) refusal on the part of leaders to work well for their followers and citizens.

Conflict between groups within countries has also been common in Africa. More than 15 million Africans have been killed in the civil wars of Africa since 1990, with more than 3 million losing their lives in Congo and more than 2 million in the Sudan. Since 2003, according to the United Nations, more than 200,000 people have been killed in an ethnic-cleansing rampage in Sudan's Darfur region. In 2007, major civil wars and other serious conflicts persisted in Burundi, the Central African Republic, Chad, the Democratic Republic of the Congo, Ivory Coast, Sudan (in addition to the mayhem in Darfur), Uganda, and Zimbabwe.

Despite such dangers, despotism, and decay, Africa is improving. Botswana and Mauritius, now joined by South Africa, Senegal, and Ghana, are beacons of democratic growth and enlightened rule. Uganda and Senegal are taking the lead in combating and reducing the spread of AIDS, and others are following. There are serious signs of the kinds of progressive economic policy changes that might lead to prosperity for more of Africa's peoples. The trajectory in Africa is positive.

The purpose of the African Union is to help lift African countries out of poverty and provide new opportunities for the continent's residents. One way the organization hopes to do this is by improving educational programs, which often lack supplies, adequate facilities, and trained teachers.

Although Africa is rich in natural resources, its people are among the world's poorest. (Opposite) A malnourished boy waits with his mother at a medical clinic in Somalia. (Right) African leaders attend a 2002 ceremony creating the African Union. The organization was formed to help alleviate the continent's many problems.

1 A Continent in Crisis Seeks New Hope

ON JULY 9, 2002, representatives of 53 African states met in Durban, South Africa, for the official inauguration of a new cooperative organization, the African Union (AU). Although the African Union has numerous objectives, the *federation*'s main goals include promoting greater economic prosperity for all Africans and ensuring freedom and the protection of human rights throughout the continent.

Africa should play an important role in world affairs: it is the world's second-largest continent, and is home to more than 900 million people. However, despite Africa's exceptional *diversity* and abundant natural resources, it remains a continent in crisis. Its people are among the world's poorest, and millions live under *authoritarian* regimes that use brutal methods to keep the citizens in line. According to a 2005 report issued by the World Bank, 29 percent of the world's poorest people—surviving on less than $1 per day—live in Africa. This figure is expected to rise to 50 percent by 2015.

The Problems of Africa

The absence of strong, diverse economies holds African countries back in many ways. For example, many governments spend little money on education, and as a result, in 15 African states fewer than half of the people can read or write. Unfortunately, a lack of education perpetuates the cycle of poverty. This is true at an individual level—the only work most uneducated Africans are qualified for is *subsistence* farming—as well as at the national level—a country without an educated workforce will find it difficult to develop its economy beyond simply supplying agricultural goods or other raw *commodities* for export and processing elsewhere.

Health care is another area that is generally underfunded in Africa. Many Africans do not have access to hospitals or medicines, so diseases that could be prevented or treated, such as AIDS, *malaria*, and *tuberculosis*, kill many people each year. Because of this the average life expectancy in Africa is just 54 years, compared to over 75 years in the United States, Japan, and other developed countries.

Constant conflict in Africa has also hampered economic development. Since the African states became independent from European control during the late 1950s and 1960s, the continent has been plagued by numerous wars. These conflicts, in places like Nigeria, Angola, Sudan,

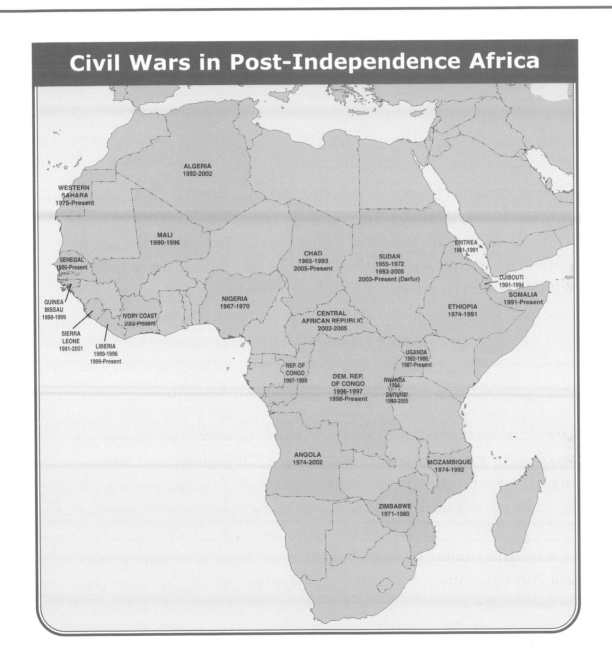

Civil Wars in Post-Independence Africa

WESTERN SAHARA
1975-Present

ALGERIA
1992-2002

MALI
1990-1996

SENEGAL
1990-Present

GUINEA BISSAU
1998-1999

SIERRA LEONE
1991-2001

IVORY COAST
2002-Present

LIBERIA
1989-1996
1999-Present

NIGERIA
1967-1970

CHAD
1965-1993
2005-Present

SUDAN
1955-1972
1983-2005
2003-Present (Darfur)

ERITREA
1961-1991

DJIBOUTI
1991-1994

SOMALIA
1991-Present

CENTRAL AFRICAN REPUBLIC
2002-2005

ETHIOPIA
1974-1991

REP. OF CONGO
1997-1999

DEM. REP. OF CONGO
1996-1997
1998-Present

UGANDA
1982-1986
1987-Present

RWANDA
1994

BURUNDI
1993-2005

ANGOLA
1974-2002

MOZAMBIQUE
1974-1992

ZIMBABWE
1971-1980

Sierra Leone, and the Democratic Republic of the Congo, are estimated to have cost more than $250 billion and to have claimed over 12 million lives. During a civil war, industries are ruined and fertile land is damaged. People are left homeless and destitute. Waging the war, and rebuilding once peace comes, diverts resources that the state might have used to build individual wealth and a stable national economy.

Many leaders have come to believe that Africa must learn how to work together peacefully if the continent is to extricate itself from its history of poverty and war. They feel that the states of Africa will be stronger collectively than they are individually, in the same way that the states of the United States of America work together for the national good. The African Union may be an early step toward this goal, allowing African countries to pool their resources and giving them greater leverage in negotiating trade agreements.

The European Union as a Model

In some respects the African Union resembles another organization of states, the European Union (EU), which was formed to promote greater fiscal and social cooperation between European states.

The idea of closer cooperation between European nations arose from the ashes of conflict. After witnessing the social and economic devastation caused by the first and second world wars, European leaders understood that their civilization could not survive another such conflict. It was believed that increased economic interdependence and a federal governing body could keep another massive war from ever happening again. In 1957 six

European leaders sign the Treaty of Rome, 1957. The decision to integrate European economies, and eventually form the European Union (EU) in 1993, has paid off for most EU member states. African leaders hoped to emulate the European Union's success by forming their own federation of states.

Most of the EU states adopted a shared currency, the Euro, in 2002. Leaders of the African Union intend for their organization to one day create a single currency for Africa, which will aid in integrating the continent's diverse economies into a single bloc.

European countries—Belgium, France, Italy, Luxembourg, the Netherlands, and West Germany—agreed to form the European Economic Community, which was intended to work toward a coordinated economy. Over time other European countries, such as Great Britain, Ireland, Denmark, Sweden, Austria, and Portugal, joined the organization, which was renamed the European Community. A new organization called the European Union, which took further steps to integrate the European countries politically and economically, was formally established with the signing of the Maastricht Treaty on November 1, 1993. A new currency, the Euro, was adopted by most EU countries in 2002 as a way to stabilize exchange rates and facilitate trade between European countries.

Because the European Union binds many smaller countries together into a single economic bloc, European companies are better able to compete with their rivals in the United States, Japan, and China. The African Union similarly hopes to one day have an integrated economy that encompasses the entire continent—one that can compete in the world market and raise Africans out of poverty.

(Opposite) Nigerian President Olusegun Obasajo (center), then serving as president of the African Union, plants a tree with President Blaise Compaoré (left) of Burkina Faso and Alpha Oumar Konare, president of the AU Commission. (Right) The Organization of African Unity, a predecessor of the AU, meets in Addis Ababa during 1966.

2 Seeking Unity for Africa

THE IDEA OF AFRICAN UNITY is not new. It originated in the 19th century, partly as a response to European colonial policies on the continent. Throughout that century the countries of Europe sought to establish colonies around the globe that could provide them with raw materials and labor to help them build economic and military empires. European powers like France, Great Britain, Germany, Belgium, Portugal, and Italy each sought a foothold in Africa.

In 1884, leaders from 14 countries, including the United States, met in Berlin for a conference on Africa. When the Berlin Conference ended in 1885, the borders of each European country's colony had been established. Unfortunately, the Europeans never bothered to consult the Africans before carving up the continent. As a result, regions were divided without any regard for the tribes or ethnic groups who lived there. For example, the Bakongo people of central Africa were divided between three new countries, all with different rulers: French Congo, Belgian Congo, and Portuguese Angola. Groups with no common history, culture, religion, or language were thrown together—in some cases, deadly enemies were expected to live peacefully together as residents of the same colony. To maintain order in the colonies among these different people, the European powers used force and repression.

The Pan-African Congresses

One of the important early moments in the history of African nationalism occurred in August 1893, when a meeting called the Congress on Africa was held in Chicago as part of that city's World's Colombian Exposition. The event, also sometimes called the Congress on African Ethnology or the Congress on the Negro, featured such African-American dignitaries as Frederick Douglass and Timothy Thomas Fortune discussing the future of Africa. Their audience consisted of well-educated blacks and whites, as well as highly respected African leaders from the continent itself.

Four years later, in 1897, an educated black man from Trinidad named Henry Sylvester Williams founded the African Association. At the time Trinidad was a British colony and Williams was studying law in London. The association's goal was to encourage cooperation between people of African descent around the world, as well as to promote the interests of African people within the British Empire. The group generated so much publicity that some members of the British parliament began to question the treatment of blacks in the empire.

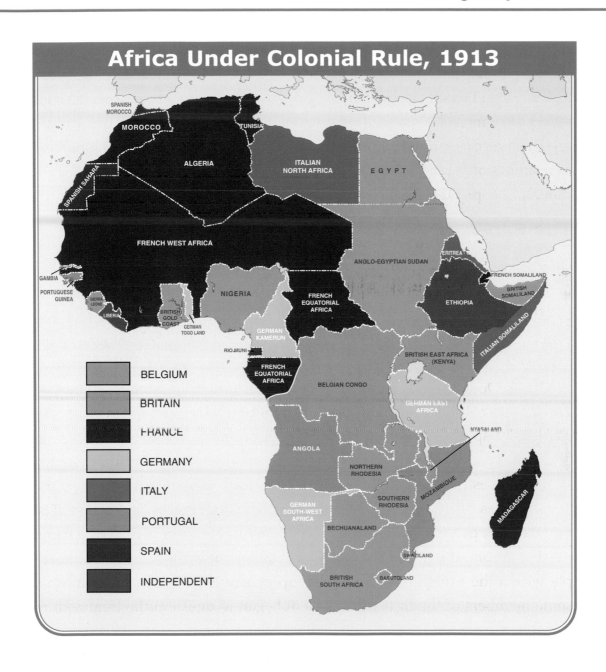

Africa Under Colonial Rule, 1913

SPANISH MOROCCO

MOROCCO

TUNISIA

SPANISH SAHARA

ALGERIA

ITALIAN NORTH AFRICA

EGYPT

FRENCH WEST AFRICA

ANGLO-EGYPTIAN SUDAN

ERITREA

FRENCH SOMALILAND

GAMBIA

PORTUGUESE GUINEA

SIERRA LEONE

LIBERIA

BRITISH GOLD COAST

GERMAN TOGO LAND

NIGERIA

FRENCH EQUATORIAL AFRICA

ETHIOPIA

BRITISH SOMALILAND

ITALIAN SOMALILAND

GERMAN KAMERUN

RIO MUNI

FRENCH EQUATORIAL AFRICA

BELGIAN CONGO

BRITISH EAST AFRICA (KENYA)

GERMAN EAST AFRICA

ANGOLA

NYASALAND

NORTHERN RHODESIA

MOZAMBIQUE

MADAGASCAR

GERMAN SOUTH-WEST AFRICA

SOUTHERN RHODESIA

BECHUANALAND

SWAZILAND

BASUTOLAND

BRITISH SOUTH AFRICA

Legend:
- BELGIUM
- BRITAIN
- FRANCE
- GERMANY
- ITALY
- PORTUGAL
- SPAIN
- INDEPENDENT

Following up on this initial success, in July 1900 Williams organized and hosted the Pan-African Conference in London. (The prefix *pan* means "all" or "everyone," so Pan-African refers to all Africans.) Thirty-seven representatives from the United States, Europe, and non-British Africa attended, including an African-American professor named W.E.B. DuBois, who was becoming internationally known for his writings about racial issues. From this London conference emerged a new organization called the Pan-African Association (PAA). The primary goal of the PAA was to fight for the rights of all people of African descent, while also improving relations between blacks and whites. Among the group's goals were influencing legislation that affected blacks; encouraging educational, industrial, and commercial enterprise among Africans; and promoting the interests of African communities all over the world.

The writer and civil rights activist W.E.B. DuBois (1868–1963) was an important advocate of Pan-Africanism. At a series of conferences, DuBois proposed that Africans should have the right to govern themselves.

With the death of Williams in 1911, the mantle of leadership passed to DuBois. In 1919, soon after the end of World War I, he helped organize another meeting, which he called the Pan-African Congress. It was attended by 57 delegates from 15 countries, including the United States and countries in Africa and the Caribbean. The congress was timed to coincide with the Paris peace conference being held by leaders of the Allied powers, who had emerged victorious from the war. Among those leaders was U.S. President Woodrow Wilson. Before the First World War ended, Wilson had given a famous speech in which he set out 14 points that he believed were required for a fair peace agreement. One of these was that all people living in colonies should have the right to govern themselves. In a petition, the Pan-African Congress asked the Allied leaders to jointly administer the former German colonies in Africa, and also to allow Africans to take part in governing their own countries as soon as possible. However, the Allies ignored both of these requests, and Britain, France, and Belgium took over control of the German colonies.

Failing To Be Heard

DuBois hosted a second Pan-African Congress in 1921. It met in several sessions in Brussels, London, and Paris. This congress issued a radical and angry essay titled "Declaration To The World" (also known as the "London Manifesto"), which accused Great Britain of encouraging ignorance among African natives and enslaving them. It also noted that the British did not allow Africans much political power in the African colonies. "[England has refused] to grant to coloured colonies those rights of self-government which it freely gives to white men," read the manifesto. The manifesto received little attention, however.

Two years later, the third Pan-African Congress was held in London and Lisbon, Portugal. It was badly organized and poorly attended. This congress repeated demands for African self-rule and called for the development of

Africa for the benefit of Africans instead of Europeans. A fourth Pan-African Congress was held in New York during 1927 and expressed similar sentiments. Again, however, little attention was paid to these congresses' demands.

Movement Toward Independence

During the 1930s and 1940s, the idea of pan-Africanism faded into the background as other issues became more prominent: a global economic depression, the rise of Nazi Germany and an aggressive military regime in Japan, and eventually the Second World War (1939–1945). During the global conflict, however, a declaration made by the governments of the United States and Great Britain encouraged those who supported pan-Africanism. Among the principles stated in this declaration, known as the Atlantic Charter, was the right of people in Africa and other places to rule themselves.

In 1945 a fifth Pan-African Congress was held in Manchester, in the northwest of England. Instead of mainly being attended by expatriated Africans and African-Americans, it included many attendees from the African continent. A large number of them were war veterans, trade unionists, and students. Nearly all of these new attendees were full of the new spirit of democracy and self-governing that had just been fought so hard for during World War II. They were ready to demand it for their own countries.

Many of the people who attended the congress would become the leaders of African liberation movements, including Kwame Nkrumah of Ghana; Hastings Banda of Malawi; the Nigerian chief Obafemi Awolowo; and Jomo Kenyatta of Kenya. They helped to write the congress's major document, titled "Declaration to the Colonial and Subject Peoples of the World." The document called on African people under colonial rule to organize and fight for freedom. Within a decade of this meeting, numerous independence movements were underway in African countries.

After the end of the Second World War, European countries found that they could no longer afford to maintain worldwide networks of colonies. As the independence movements in Africa grew, the Europeans began granting freedom to their colonies. In March 1957 the British colony known as the Gold Coast became the independent state of Ghana, with Nkrumah serving

Kwame Nkrumah (center) is surrounded by Ghanian leaders at the March 1, 1957, ceremony in which the country gained its independence from Great Britain. The rest of Africa would throw off European rule by the 1970s.

as its first president. Guinea became independent in 1958. The French colonial territories of West Africa, such as Senegal, Mali, and Côte d'Ivoire, became independent (but still maintained links to France) in 1960. Belgium offered the Congo independence in 1960 after a riot in 1959. Nigeria also gained independence in 1960—the result of diplomatic efforts and negotiations with the British. The following year Tanzania and Sierra Leone gained their freedom, followed by Uganda, Kenya, Botswana, Swaziland, and Mauritius. By the late 1970s all of the European countries had withdrawn from their African colonies.

The Organization of African Unity

Once the goal of independence for African states was achieved, those leaders who believed in uniting the continent politically and economically were ready to take the next step. This turned out to be the formation of an organization called the Organization of African Unity (OAU) on May 25, 1963. It was based at Addis Ababa, Ethiopia's capital and largest city, at the invitation of Ethiopian Emperor Haile Selassie, who also served as the OAU's first chairman.

Thirty-three African countries initially joined the OAU. As other nations gained their independence they joined as well, with the last one being South Africa in 1994 after the end of that state's *apartheid* system and the election of Nelson Mandela as president. Ultimately, 53 of the 54 African countries became members of the OAU. (Morocco withdrew from the OAU in protest when the organization recognized the Sahrawi Arab Democratic Republic as the legitimate government of the territory known as Western Sahara—a region that Morocco claimed sovereignty over.)

One purpose of the OAU was to eliminate the influence of the colonial powers in Africa. It established a Liberation Committee to help fledgling independence movements in their fight for freedom. But from its inception, the group was divided over the extent to which the OAU should speak for its members. Some African leaders, like Nkrumah of Ghana and Gamael Nasser of Egypt, wanted even closer unification among the African countries—in effect, a central government for the entire continent. They argued that the boundaries of African countries had been artificially set by Europeans during the Berlin Conference, and should be eliminated altogether. However, other African leaders like Felix Houphouët-Boigny of the Ivory Coast argued that countries that had finally thrown off the yoke of colonialism needed to become strong individual nations before they could give up power to a continent-wide government. Ultimately, this view prevailed, and the OAU did not become a central governing body for Africa.

Article 3 of the OAU Charter, which stated that the group's members would practice "non-interference in the internal affairs of [other African] states," outlined the essential problem with the organization. The Organization of African Unity was ineffective in times of crisis because although delegates discussed the issues, the OAU rarely took action to end conflicts. Without having to worry about interference from their neighbors, African dictators could do whatever they wanted within their own borders. As a result, the OAU was sometimes referred to as the "dictator's club."

The organization did successfully negotiate border disagreements between Algeria and Morocco, as well as between Somalia, Ethiopia, and Kenya. It also sent a peacekeeping force to Chad in 1981 as part of an effort to

The bodies of some of the more than 800,000 Rwandans killed during a three-month period in 1994 are wrapped in straw mats and piled on the side of a road. The OAU was criticized for its inability to prevent the genocide in Rwanda, as well as its unwillingness to confront dictators using repressive ruling methods in other African countries.

end that country's civil war. However, the OAU is remembered most for what it did *not* do to prevent the many conflicts that have swept across Africa since the mid-1960s. Nigeria, Sudan, Zaire (now the Democratic Republic of the Congo), Angola, Somalia, Liberia, Rwanda, Burundi, and others were ravaged by wars that killed millions of innocent people while the OAU maintained its policy of non-interference.

The Rwandan *genocide* of 1994, pitting Hutu against Tutsi in a rage of ethnic killing in which more than 800,000 people were massacred in just three months, was an example of the OAU's inability to react to crisis. The organization proved unable to help stop Tutsi and moderate Hutu from being murdered, and was also unable to convince the United Nations, the United States, the European Union, or any other country or group with greater resources to get involved in halting the slaughter.

The Sirte Declaration of 1999

As the 20th century neared a close, Libyan leader Muammar al-Gaddafi began encouraging other African leaders to work toward a united Africa. He urged the creation of a new African organization based upon the model of the United States of America—in essence, a United States of Africa, complete with an African Congress that would establish laws for the continent. In September 1999 he invited African leaders to the Libyan seaside city of Sirte to discuss his vision.

At first the Sirte conference seemed unlikely to succeed. Many delegates felt that, given Africa's economic problems, history of conflict, and broad ethnic diversity, true unity was unrealistic. But the Sirte conference emphasized

Libyan leader Muammar al-Gaddafi delivers a speech in July 2002 at the ceremony marking the official launch of the African Union. Gaddafi had long expounded the view that African countries should unite politically. In 1999, at a special OAU session held in the Libyan city of Sirte, the foundations of the African Union were established.

the desirability of closer political and economic relations between African nations, and eventually these arguments won out. Representatives of all 53 OAU member states that attended the Sirte conference signed the Constitutive Act of African Union, better known as the Sirte Declaration, which established a framework upon which the African Union could operate. By the end of the conference, 31 African states had already *ratified* the Constitutive Act. Many agreed with Algerian President Abdelaziz Bouteflika, who said, "We have to secure peace and stability in Africa. This is the only way for us to move forward."

In July 2000 at an OAU summit in Lomé in the West African nation of Togo, the Constitutive Act of the African Union was formally adopted. At that time it was anticipated that it would require two years for the African Union to be formed. A second summit, in 2001 at Lusaka, Zambia, adopted a plan for launching the AU the following year at Durban. At the Durban conference in 2002 the OAU was formally disbanded and replaced by the AU.

The basic framework of the African Union is contained in the Constitutive Act. However, many AU bodies have not yet been formed. (Opposite) Patrick Mazimhaka (right), deputy chairman of the AU Commission, stands with foreign leaders at the opening of a 2007 summit in Addis Ababa. (Right) Alpha Oumar Konare was elected head of the AU Commission in 2003.

3 Organization of the African Union

THE CONSTITUTIVE ACT, which created the framework for the AU, includes provisions for many governmental bodies (or *organs*). To date, only four of these organs have been launched: the Assembly, the Executive Council, the Permanent Representatives Committee, and the AU Commission. The structures of other governmental bodies, including a continent-wide court system, are currently being developed.

The Assembly

The Assembly is the main decision-making body of the AU, and is composed of the head of state from each member nation. It is presided over by a chairperson who is elected for a one-year term. Normally, the head of the country that hosts the annual AU meeting assumes the leadership of the organization.

According to the Constitutive Act, the Assembly must meet at least once a year. The first meeting of the Assembly was held during July 2002 in Durban, South Africa. That country's president, Thabo Mbeki, was also the African Union's first chairperson. Subsequent annual meetings have been held in various cities throughout Africa. However, the assembly can also be called into extraordinary session at the request of any member if the request is approved by a two-thirds majority vote.

African leaders attend the official opening of the AU Assembly.

Goals of the African Union

The members of the African Union established numerous objectives when the federation was established. These objectives include:

- To achieve greater unity and solidarity between African countries and African peoples;
- To defend the self-government, territorial completeness, and independence of its members;
- To speed up Africa's political, social, and economic development;
- To promote and defend African positions on issues that affect the continent and its people;
- To encourage international cooperation;
- To promote the peace, security, and stability of African countries;
- To advocate democratic principles, institutions, and good governments, as well as the people's participation in the process of good government;
- To promote and protect human rights;
- To make Africa a participant in world issues and in the international economy;
- To help the advancement of social, economic, and cultural conditions while merging the economies of African nations;
- To raise the living standards of the African people;
- To work with the policies of the five Regional Economic Communities;
- To encourage research and development in science and technology; and
- To promote good health and try to wipe out preventable diseases.

As the African Union's main body, the Assembly can take action on whatever matters are before it. Among the Assembly's most important functions are adopting the organization's budget; determining what policies the AU is going to implement; entertaining requests and proposals by AU members; and considering reports and recommendations made by other departments of the African Union.

The Executive Council and Permanent Representatives Committee

The Executive Council is made up of the foreign ministers of the AU member states. This body is scheduled to meet at least twice a year in ordinary session; however, any member can ask for a special session (this requires two-thirds of the council members to vote in favor of the request).

The Executive Council develops policies on important issues that affect all member nations, such as foreign trade, agriculture, and communications. It reports on these issues to the Assembly, which must vote to approve the policies. Assisting the Executive Council in these duties is the Permanent Representatives Council, which consists of delegates nominated by the AU members. The PRC's functions include setting the agenda for Executive Council meetings and monitoring the AU's budget.

The AU Commission

The AU Commission is the administrative arm of the African Union, and is responsible for keeping the organization operating smoothly. It prepares strategic plans and studies for the Executive Council to consider; develops and coordinates AU programs with the Regional Economic Communities (RECs); and represents the African Union in negotiations and discussions with member states.

In addition to a chairperson and vice chairperson, there are eight commissioners. Each member of the AU Commission oversees a government department or policy area. These include:

- Conferences and Events
- Peace and Security
- Political Affairs
- Infrastructure and Energy
- Social Affairs
- Human Resources, Science and Technology
- Trade and Industry
- Rural Economy and Agriculture
- Economic Affairs
- Legal Council

Alpha Oumar Konare, the former president of Mali, was elected chairman in 2003. The deputy chairperson of the AU Commission is Patrick Mazimhaka of Rwanda.

The Pan-African Parliament

The Pan-African Parliament is one of several governmental organs that are not yet fully functioning. The Parliament currently serves as a *consultative* and advisory body; however, according to the Constitutive Act, it will eventually possess full legislative powers and become the ultimate lawmaking body of the African Union.

Gertrude Mongela was elected president of the Pan-African Parliament in 2004. The Tanzanian previously served as an assistant secretary-general of the United Nations.

According to the Constitutive Act, each AU member can provide five representatives, one of whom must be a woman. This would give the parliament 265 members, with 20 percent of them women. This is in keeping with the AU's intention of promoting the rights and interests of African women. Members of this parliament are members of the legislative bodies in their home counties, and their tenure in the Pan-African Parliament lasts as long as they are in office in their country.

The initial session of the Pan-African Parliament was held on March 18, 2004, at Addis Ababa, Ethiopia. At that time the assembly was composed of 202 legislators, representing 41 of the 53 AU members. Gertrude Mongela of Tanzania was elected as the Pan-African Parliament's first president, to serve a five-year term. The parliament later moved to a permanent home in Midrand, South Africa.

Judicial System

The Constitutive Act also called for the establishment of an African Court of Justice. This court, which has not yet been formed, will eventually consist of

Languages, Emblem and Flag

The official policy of the African Union is to promote the use of African languages in its work. Official languages used by the organization are Arabic, English, French, Kiswahili, and Portuguese. All African languages are considered working languages by the Union.

The AU emblem contains interlocking red rings inside of a gold ribbon. Palm leaves, representing peace, come up from both sides of the ribbon and flank an outer circle of gold and inner green circle. Inside the inner circle is the African continent without the divisions for individual countries, representing African unity. The gold circle symbolizes Africa's wealth, the green circle stands for Africa's hopes and dreams, and the interlocking red rings represent unity and the blood shed for the continent's liberation.

The flag of the African Union is similar to the emblem. It consists of two broad green stripes on the top and bottom (again symbolizing hope), two narrower gold stripes that represent Africa's wealth, and a broad white stripe in the middle that contains the African emblem. The white stripe indicates Africa's pure desire to have friends throughout the world.

11 judges elected by the Assembly for either four- or six-year terms. The Court of Justice will have jurisdiction over all disputes related to the African Union, including treaties, decisions by the Assembly and other organs, or disagreements between state members of the AU.

A continent-wide court is already operating—the African Court on Human and Peoples' Rights, formed as a result of an AU mandate. The purpose of this court is to determine whether the AU member states are in compliance with a treaty called the Banjul Charter, which was intended to protect human rights and basic freedoms in Africa. The 11 judges of the African Court on Human and Peoples' Rights held their first session during July 2006 in Arusha, Tanzania.

The Constitutive Act requires that a percentage of leadership positions in the African Union be reserved for women, in order to promote greater equality on the continent. Pictured are two female members of the AU Commission at a 2007 meeting, Rosebud Kurwijila of Tanzania and Dr. Nagia Essayed of Libya.

AU leaders intend to eventually integrate these two courts as the Union's judicial branch. However, the level of integration must still be determined. If the courts were to be integrated on all levels, the Constitutive Act would have to be rewritten. An alternate solution would be for the two courts to function separately, but share some administrative and secretarial functions to reduce operating costs.

African Union Anthem

The African Union has its own anthem. The words, listed below, talk about Africa as the cradle of mankind and also of Africa's struggle.

Let us all unite and celebrate together
The victories won for our liberation
Let us dedicate ourselves to rise together
To defend our liberty and unity

O Sons and Daughters of Africa
Flesh of the Sun and Flesh of the Sky
Let us make Africa the Tree of Life

Let us all unite and sing together
To uphold the bonds that frame our destiny
Let us dedicate ourselves to fight together
For lasting peace and justice on earth

O Sons and Daughters of Africa
Flesh of the Sun and Flesh of the Sky
Let us make Africa the Tree of Life

Let us all unite and toil together
To give the best we have to Africa
The cradle of mankind and fount of culture
Our pride and hope at break of dawn.

O Sons and Daughters of Africa
Flesh of the Sun and Flesh of the Sky
Let us make Africa the Tree of Life

Advisory Bodies

The Constitutive Act also included provisions for several advisory bodies, which are supposed to work with the Assembly, Executive Council, and Commission. These include the Peace and Security Council, the Economic, Social and Cultural Council, and seven Specialized Technical Committees.

The Peace and Security Council, which is responsible for enforcing AU decisions, is similar in some ways to the U.N. Security Council. Fifteen countries, chosen to reflect regional diversity, are represented in the council. Ten countries are elected for two-year terms, while five are elected for three-year periods.

Unlike the Organization of African Unity, the African Union has authority to *intervene* in the affairs of African countries. To that end, the Peace and Security Council is responsible for to evaluating potential trouble spots, suggesting AU intervention if necessary, and then coordinating the activities of peacekeeping troops. At the 2004 ceremony inaugurating the Peace and Security Council, Mozambique's President Joaquim Chissano, who was serving as chairman of the African Union at the time, commented:

> The Peace and Security Council has been designed to be a strong signal to the African peoples and the international community of our determination to put an end to the conflicts and wars which have ravaged the continent for far too long.

In addition to stopping or preventing conflicts in Africa, which the OAU proved woefully unable to do, the framers of the Constitutive Act wanted the African Union to have closer links to the people of the continent. The OAU

Joaquim Chissano speaks at the formal launch of the AU's Peace and Security Council in May 2004. By giving the Peace and Security Council a mandate to intervene in conflict areas, the African Union hopes it will improve stability in the continent.

was roundly criticized as a collection of rulers that did not represent the interests of the people, whose lives were too often disrupted by war, disease, famine, and political repression. The Economic, Social and Cultural Council (ECOSOCC) is the AU organ intended to establish links to the people. When it is formed, ECOSOCC will communicate with trade unions, commercial associations, and other groups to make sure their interests are represented to the government. It will also act as an advisory council for projects that other AU organs plan to implement.

The African Union's seven Specialized Technical Committees each deal with a specific area, including:

- Rural Economy and Agricultural Matters
- Monetary and Financial Affairs
- Trade, Customs and Immigration
- Industry, Science and Technology, Energy, Natural Resources and Environment
- Transport, Communications and Tourism
- Health, Labor and Social Affairs
- Education, Culture and Human Resources

The committees formulate projects and submit them to the Executive Council for discussion and approval. They also conduct investigations and write reports at the direction of the Executive Council.

Financial Institutions

An important reason for the creation of the African Union is to improve the economic power of African countries. To this end, the AU intends to create three financial institutions. These will ultimately help to establish an AU currency, and will assist member states in dealing with financial matters. The three financial institutions are the African Central Bank, the African Monetary Fund, and the African Investment Bank.

The African Central Bank is scheduled to be created by 2020. When it comes into existence, the Central Bank will issue a single currency for AU members. This will be a key step in the integration of African economies, and should act as a check on the rate of *inflation*. The Central Bank will also set official interest rates and currency exchange rates, and will regulate the banking industry in Africa.

The African Investment Bank and African Monetary Fund will make loans and provide financial assistance to African countries. They will be similar to such global lending organizations as the International Monetary Fund (IMF) and the World Bank. Although both the IMF and World Bank currently finance projects in Africa, many African leaders feel that AU-based lending organizations would be less likely to impose what they view as unfair conditions on the receipt of funds. In addition, the African Monetary Fund would have a department that would help AU members negotiate for better terms on IMF or World Bank loans.

A major challenge for the African Investment Bank and African Monetary Fund will be finding the funds to get started. Each African country will have to invest in these financial institutions, and AU leaders also hope that wealthy countries like Saudi Arabia, China, and the United States, which have an interest in Africa's economic growth, will also provide funding.

Africa faces many challenges, and it remains uncertain that the African Union will be able to resolve any of them. (Opposite) A member of the AU peacekeeping force in war-torn Darfur takes part in a patrol through the village of Tawilah. (Right) Protestors demand that Western countries forgive African debt outside an AU session in South Africa.

4 Challenges Faced by the African Union

THE AU FACES ENORMOUS CHALLENGES in its quest to unite Africa and transform it into an economic and political power. Perhaps no other continent on earth faces the war, poverty, disease, famine, inadequate educational facilities, and poor health care that Africa does. Fixing any one of these would be a difficult task; handling all at once has so far proven impossible.

Ending Conflict in Africa

Stopping and preventing wars will be one of the AU's greatest challenges. The wars of liberation that raged across Africa as it freed itself from colonialism have been replaced by conflicts pitting nations against one another, ethnic groups against each other, and sometimes, even governments against their own people. The AU hopes having its own 15,000-member peacekeeping force ready to step in when necessary will help bring stability to the continent.

AU peacekeepers have already accepted several missions. In 2003 troops from South Africa, Mozambique, and Ethiopia were sent to Burundi to ensure the safe installment of that country's new transitional government. The African Union troops were eventually relieved by UN peacekeepers, who themselves are now leaving the country.

The AU has also attempted to resolve an ethnic conflict in the Darfur region of Sudan. In July 2004 the African Union, along with the European Union, sent monitors into Darfur to make sure a ceasefire agreement signed in April 2004 between the two warring sides was being observed. The AU eventually sent 300 soldiers from Rwanda and Nigeria to protect the monitors; these peacekeepers were authorized to intervene and protect civilians if necessary. By February 2006 the number of AU troops had increased to 7,000. Most of the soldiers were from Nigeria, Senegal, the Gambia, Kenya, and South Africa.

While the peacekeepers attempted to end fighting between the various factions, the African Union also sponsored a series of peace talks aimed at ending the conflict. In May 2006 talks in Abuja, Nigeria, resulted in a peace agreement signed by the Sudanese government and one of the rebel groups. However, other rebel factions were not a part of the agreement, and the ceasefire's future is uncertain. The violence in Darfur has claimed the lives of more than 400,000, and forced more than 2 million people to leave their homes.

In June 2006 at the AU summit in Banjul, the Gambia, the African Union decided to keep its peacekeepers in Darfur until the end of 2006, when the

United Nations was scheduled to take over the peacekeeping role. However, the government of Sudan has refused to allow the UN peacekeeping force into Darfur. As a result, the AU force has remained in the country longer than originally intended.

The African Union has also responded to political unrest in other countries. For example, the AU intervened when a 2003 *coup* overthrew the government of the Central African Republic. It opened an office in Bangui, the capital, to help ensure free and fair elections were held. Similarly, when Faure Gnassingbe attempted to seize power in Togo during February 2005, the AU

AU leaders meet with West African diplomats to discuss the situation in Togo, May 2005. The African Union declared that an attempt by Faure Gnassingbe to seize power was an illegal coup, and pressured Gnassingbe to resign and hold an election to determine the country's president.

quickly declared his actions an illegal coup and helped to bring about a new election. Although Gnassingbe won that election, there have been questions about its fairness, and the AU has been involved in trying to help form a legitimate coalition government. These kinds of interventions would never have happened with the Organization of African Unity.

Protecting Human Rights

One of the stated goals of the African Union is the protection of human rights on the continent. This is something that has been a problem historically in many African regimes. To that end, the AU established the new African Court on Human and Peoples' Rights (ACHPR). It also mandates that women be fully represented in the African Union, as well as in the governments of member states.

Unfortunately, the AU's record on human-rights issues has been mixed so far, as seen in its lack of response to alleged abuses by Zimbabwe's government. Strongman Robert Mugabe has ruled Zimbabwe since 1980; most international observers agree his policies have led to the country's economic collapse. Today more than 80 percent of Zimbabwe's population is unemployed, inflation is over 1000 percent, the country is deeply in debt, and over 65 percent of the people live below the poverty line. Political repression and human-rights abuses are common in Zimbabwe, yet the African Union has never taken action against the dictator.

One of the first significant cases to come before the ACHPR was that of Gabriel Shumba, a lawyer from Zimbabwe. After Shumba appeared in court to defend a member of a group that opposed the Mugabe government, he was arrested in January 2003. Shumba was not informed of the charges against him, and during his three-day imprisonment he was starved and tortured with chemicals and electricity. After he was released, Shumba eventually asked the African Court on Human and Peoples' Rights to hear his case. But although his claims of torture were authenticated by numerous international organizations, the ACHPR continually delayed his case. Some say that this proves the AU will do as little to prevent human rights' abuses in Africa as did the OAU.

Supporting this pessimism is a July 2004 report about abuses in Zimbabwe presented to the African Union Assembly by the AU's Commission on Human and Peoples' Rights. The adoption of the report (to adopt a report is to accept it as factual and perhaps worthy of action) was postponed when Zimbabwe's representative protested. When the report was finally adopted in January 2005 the AU decided not to publish the report until Zimbabwe's government had a chance to respond to the allegations it contained.

Another case in Zimbabwe that has received little attention from the African Union is Mugabe's controversial Operation Murambatsvina (Drive Out the Trash) program. The government claims that the program is intended to reduce the spread of infectious diseases by targeting illegal housing and commercial activities in slum areas. However, a report by UN Special Envoy Anna Tibaijuka indicated that the program may be revenge against those living in poor areas who voted for the opposition party Movement for Democratic Change in the last election. International organizations have called for the program to cease, and the African Union sent Alpha Oumar Konare, the chairman of the AU Commission, on a fact-finding mission in

A house is torn down in Chitungwiza, Zimbabwe, as part of President Mugabe's controversial "Drive out the Trash" campaign. Critics of the Mugabe regime claim the program targeted the dwellings of the president's political opponents.

2005. However, since Konare's return the AU has done nothing, claiming that there are more important matters that need its attention. This has led some to feel that the AU, like its predecessor the OAU, is not going to stand up to dictators in cases where human rights violations are suspected.

Combating AIDS and Famine

Another problem facing the continent—particularly sub-Saharan Africa—is the deadly disease AIDS. According to statistics from the organization UNAIDS, which is tracking the global AIDS epidemic, in 2006 some 24.7 million Africans were infected with HIV, the virus that causes AIDS—63 percent of the global total infected with the disease. Of the 4.3 million new infections worldwide during 2006, 2.8 million (65 percent) occurred in sub-Saharan Africa. In 2006 2.9 million people died of AIDS, with 2.1 million deaths (72 percent) occurring in sub-Saharan Africa.

AIDS creates a huge drain on all facets of the African economy. African governments spend millions of dollars each year on treatment programs and health care facilities. Individual workers with AIDS are removed from the employment pool, and often there are no trained workers to take their places. For example, the World Food Programme trained 40 engineers to streamline the roadway system in Kenya, so that food could be distributed more efficiently and effectively. However, before the project was completed 36 of the engineers had died of AIDS. Additionally, when someone becomes sick with AIDS other members of the family must care for him or her, leaving fewer people able to earn money in the workplace and support the family.

The great number of deaths, particularly among Africans who practice subsistence farming, has caused the United Nations to coin a new term, *new variant famine*. This is a famine that is not caused by traditional problems such as droughts, floods, or insect infestations, and as a result traditional solutions are useless. There is no way to compensate from the loss of manpower caused

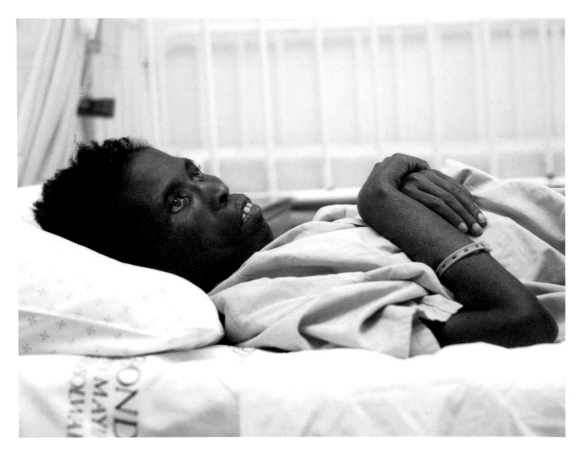

AIDS is the leading cause of death in sub-Saharan Africa. It is particularly prevalent in the southern part of the continent. In South Africa, the home of this infected woman, nearly 20 percent of the people between the ages of 15 and 49 are believed to be HIV-positive.

by the AIDS epidemic, and those who remain often do not have the skills or knowledge to produce enough food. Additionally, during a traditional famine adults would give up food and instead feed the more vulnerable children. In a family where one or more people are infected with AIDS, the adult can no longer provide for the children, so the effect of the new variant famine is exacerbated.

Famine does not require AIDS to be a terrible killer. By itself, famine is killing millions of Africans in countries like Niger, Mali, Mauritania, Eritrea, Ethiopia, Burkina Faso, and Zimbabwe. According to the World Food Programme, in 2006 more than 200 million Africans suffered from malnutrition and some 40 million were in danger of starvation.

Promoting Good Governance

African countries possess many natural resources, including diamonds, oil, timber, uranium, and gold. For centuries, these resources have attracted foreign investment; however, the wealth that natural resources bring when sold often does not reach the people of the country that sold it. Typically, the money generated goes to the government—and in many cases, it winds up in the bank account of that country's ruler or his cronies. This has resulted in an incredible paradox: some of the richest countries in the world in terms of natural resources are also some of the poorest in the world in terms of the standard of living for their people.

In order for the people of Africa to prosper, there must be a balance between economic interests and the public good. Unfortunately, government corruption is one of the leading problems in Africa. The OAU turned a blind eye when rulers like Gnassingbe Eyadema of Togo, Sani Abacha of Nigeria, and Mobutu Sese Seko of Zaire stole money from their countries that could have been used for development, health care, education, and many other needs. More recently, Equatorial Guinea successfully increased its oil production to generate more income; as a result its **gross domestic product** (GDP) rose from $328 million in 1995 to $25.7 billion in 2006. However, there was no accompanying rise in the living standards of most of the country's people. Because of concerns about government corruption, the World Bank and International Monetary Fund cut off some financial assistance programs to Equatorial Guinea.

Unfortunately, the example of Equatorial Guinea is not an isolated case. The international organization Transparency International, which produces an annual index of the world's most corrupt countries, found in a 2006 poll that 56 percent of Africans believe their countries are unable to prevent bribes and other official misbehavior. A 2002 African Union report estimated the cost of government corruption at nearly $150 billion a year. This increases the cost of goods by up to 20 percent and deters foreign investment in the country. Most of the cost, the AU report found, falls on the poor.

To resolve the issue of government corruption, the African Union has proposed a convention that would force public officials to declare their assets when they take office. The government would have the authority to seize bank records and other documents in order to track cases in which public officials are suspected of fraud or accepting bribes. Those convicted of corrupt practices would have their personal assets confiscated.

Through the Constitutive Act, the African Union has also declared its intent not to support regimes that assume governmental power through violent coups or illegitimate means. The act says, "governments which shall come to power through unconstitutional means shall not be allowed to participate in the activities of the Union." AU members will impose sanctions against such rogue governments, and the African Union will also lobby other countries and international organizations like the United Nations to impose sanctions. The AU has also deployed troops to prevent such forcible takeovers.

Encouraging Economic Development

The African Union helps to administer a program that is intended to encourage economic development in African countries. The New Partnership for Africa's Development (NEPAD) was launched in 2001 as a

African heads of state pose for a photograph after a meeting of the New Partnership for Africa's Development (NEPAD).

partnership between African countries and industrialized nations. NEPAD promised that African leaders would work on economic reforms, uphold democratic principles, and strive to follow good governance policies in exchange for fair trade policies, investment, and aid and debt relief from the wealthier countries.

NEPAD programs focus primarily on agriculture, the development of *infrastructure*, and on improving access to African markets. The organization also pursues improvements to the health care and educational systems of African countries. For example, in 2003 NEPAD launched a plan to provide computers and internet access to all high schools in Africa within five years, and to all schools within 10 years. The organization is working with Western companies like Hewlett-Packard to reach this goal.

One issue that retards economic development in Africa, and has attracted much public attention in recent years, is the problem of debt. When countries borrow money from the International Monetary Fund, the World Bank, or from other countries, they must repay that money with interest. Unfortunately, many African countries are still repaying debts from unsuccessful projects started during the 1970s and 1980s. The UN Conference on Trade and Development recently determined that during a 32-year period, African countries received $540 billion in loans. Although the countries had repaid over $550 billion to date, they still owed $295 billion because of the interest on the loans.

For countries with struggling economies, such as Cameroon, high debt payments take away money that could be used for economic and social development. At the turn of the 21st century Cameroon was making $280 million in debt payments each year, while spending just $239 million on education and $87 million on health care. In other countries, the people are paying for bad decisions made by their leaders. For example, Mobutu Sese Seko stole more than $5 billion in aid money provided by the International Monetary Fund (IMF) to Zaire. Although the citizens of Mobutu's country (now the Democratic Republic of the Congo) never received any benefit from that loan, they are still required to repay the debt.

In 2005 the IMF proposed the Multilateral Debt Relief Initiative (MDRI). This advocated 100 percent relief on eligible debt owed to the IMF, the International Development Association of the World Bank, and the African Development Fund for nearly two dozen poor nations. Many of those nations were in Africa, including Ethiopia, Ghana, Mozambique, Rwanda, and Zambia.

However, merely wiping out a country's debt does not guarantee that it will become prosperous. A corrupt government can still steal the nation's profits

As ruler of Zaire (now the Democratic Republic of the Congo) from 1965 to 1997, dictator Mobutu Sese Seko diverted public funds into his private Swiss bank accounts, amassing an enormous personal fortune estimated at over $5 billion and driving his country deeply into debt. To prevent this type of theft from occurring in the future, the African Union has pledged to promote good governance and fight corruption.

instead of investing it back into the country. The AU must come up with a system for monitoring debt relief so that it can assure that any savings are being used to benefit the entire population.

The Challenge of Funding the African Union

To accomplish the goals that the African Union has set, such as sponsoring peacekeeping missions, fighting disease and government corruption, and helping African countries to grow economically, the organization requires a sizable budget. All of these objectives take significant amounts of money. Simply finding funding for all these goals is a major challenge. In 2004 AU Commission Chairman Alpha Oumar Konare asked the member states to provide $600 million in funding for the next year; ultimately, a budget of $158 million was approved. That budget allocated $63 million to cover the cost of running the African Union, and $95 million for various programs. The budget for 2006 was even lower, at $129 million.

Collecting the money owed by member states has also been a problem. A 2006 report by Dr. Maxwell M. Mkwezalamba, the AU's commissioner for economic affairs, found that only about 57 percent of the contributions owed by member states for 2005 had been collected by the end of that year.

Some foreign nations, including the United States and Great Britain, have contributed funds to help the African Union operate. Another source of funding might be Africans who are living in other countries. The magazine *Business Day Nigeria* reports that there are approximately 5 million Nigerians in Europe and North America who could contribute up to $15 billion dollars to African projects.

Conclusion

People greeted the establishment of the African Union with mixed feelings. After the many failures of the OAU, the African Union seemed to be promising a new day for Africans on the continent. But the OAU had made its share of promises as well, so many people have reserved judgment on the AU. They are waiting to see whether the African Union's actions will live up to its promises. Only time will tell if the African Union truly represents a new beginning for Africa and its people or if it is just another dead-end.

A Calendar of African Festivals

Festivals and celebrations are a major part of life in Africa. Every ethnic group, as well as every country, has its own particular celebrations and holidays. Other celebrations are common to many parts of this vast continent. Below is a sampling of some of Africa's most important festivals.

January

New Year's Day is a holiday in many African countries, even those that do not follow the Western calendar. January 1 also is **Independence Day** in Sudan. **Epiphany**, a Christian holiday celebrating the baptism of Christ, is observed by Christian communities throughout the continent. In Ethiopia, Epiphany is known as **Timkat**, and is one of the most important celebrations of the Ethiopian Orthodox Church. In early January, Mali celebrates the annual **Festival du Desert** (Festival of the Desert), an international celebration of music and dancing held in Timbuktu. In Mauritius, which has a large Chinese community, the **Chinese New Year** is held on January 22.

February

Africa's largest annual film festival, the **Fespaco Film Festival**, is held in late February in Ouagadougou, Burkina Faso. In the Muslim areas of Nigeria, the annual **Durbar Festival** commemorates the glories of the former Muslim emirate of northern Nigeria. On the island of Zanzibar (part of Tanzania), the annual **Swahili Music and Culture Festival** is held on a three-day weekend in mid-February. It features Swahili music, theater, and dance. In Egypt, the **Abu Simbel Festival**, held on February 22 and December 22 at the ancient temple of the same name, is celebrated on the two days of the year that the sun shines directly upon the temple's shrine.

March

March 20 is Tunisia's **Independence Day**. The annual **Carnaval de Bouaké** in Ivory Coast has become one of Africa's largest festivities. It is an opportunity for the residents of Bouaké to show off their city and its culture. The carnival includes musical performances, culinary events, and an agricultural fair. The **Kilimanjaro Marathon** is held every March in Tanzania, attracting runners from around the world.

April

April 4 is Senegal's **Independence Day**. April 24, **Freedom Day**, is a major holiday in South Africa. In Mali, the **Fete des Masques** is a celebration of the mask-making tradition of the country's Dogon people.

May

Like much of the world, many African countries celebrate **Labor Day** as a public holiday on May 1. **Mawlid al-Nabiy**, the commemoration of the birthday of the prophet Muhammad, is a Muslim holiday celebrated by prayer and often a procession to the local mosque. The **Aboakyer Festival**, held in the villages of central Ghana, celebrates the migration of the Wineba people from Sudan to Ghana. The **South Sinai Camel Festival** in Egypt features camel races.

June

The annual **Festival of the Dhow Countries**, held in Zanzibar, celebrates the culture of the Muslim seafarers of the Indian Ocean. The **World Festival of Sacred Music**, held each year in Fez, Morocco, features diverse religious musical performances from around the world.

July

Independence Day is celebrated in Somalia, Burundi, and Rwanda on July 1, in Malawi on July 6, and in Liberia on July 26. Egyptians celebrate **Revolution Day** on July 23. The **Panafest** is a celebration of African performing arts held in Ghana.

64

A Calendar of African Festivals

August

August 1 is **National Day** in Benin, and August 11 is **Independence Day** in Chad. The **Homowo Festival** is an annual harvest celebration in Ghana. The **International Camel Derby and Festival**, held in Kenya, features a long camel race as well as music and other events.

September

The **Imilchil Wedding Festival** in Morocco is a unique event in which young men and women gather in the village of Imilchil and brides choose their grooms. The **Hermanus Whale Festival** in South Africa is a celebration of nature featuring whale-watching, music, food, and performances.

October

October 1 is **Independence Day** in Nigeria and October 2 in Guinea. **Fete de l'Abissa** is a weeklong carnival held in the former colonial capital and beach resort of Grand Bassam in Ivory Coast. The **Cairo Film Festival** is the most important film event in the Arab world.

November

Among Christian communities, November 1 is **All Saints' Day**, a holiday honoring all of the church's saints. The village of Man in Ivory Coast is the scene of the annual **Fetes des Masques** (Festival of Masks). The **Mombasa Carnival**, in Kenya, features parades with floats representing each of Kenya's many cultural influences.

December

The **Crossing of the Cattle** is an important holiday in Mali, honoring the cattle herders who spend most of the year seeking grazing grounds. **Incwala**, a holiday celebrated in Swaziland, kicks off the harvest season with religious and family celebrations. Africa's Christians celebrate **Christmas Day** on December 25 with church services and family gatherings. It also is a national holiday in many countries.

Other Religious Celebrations

African Muslims and Christians observe a number of important holy days related to their religions. Some of these, such as Christmas, are on particular days each year. However, many other major celebrations are held according to a lunar calendar, in which the months correspond to the phases of the moon. A lunar month is shorter than a typical month of the Western calendar. Therefore, the festival dates vary from year to year. Other celebrations are observed seasonally.

Ramadan is a month-long Muslim holiday during which time devout Muslims fast and pray throughout the daylight hours. It is the holiest period in Islam. As soon as the sun goes down, families and friends gather in homes for a meal marking the end of the fasting day. At the end of Ramadan, Muslims celebrate a major holiday called **Eid al-Fitr** (Festival of the Breaking of the Fast). This is a joyous time characterized by feasts and the exchange of gifts.

Eid al-Adha (Feast of Sacrifice) takes place in the last month of the Muslim calendar during the hajj period, when Muslims make a pilgrimage to Mecca. The holiday honors the prophet Abraham, who was willing to sacrifice his own son to Allah. Each of these holidays is celebrated with a feast. On Eid al-Adha, families traditionally eat a third of the feast and donate the rest to the poor.

The major Christian festivals on the lunar cycle involve the suffering and death of Jesus Christ. **Ash Wednesday** marks the start of a period of self-sacrifice called **Lent**, which lasts for 40 days. The final eight days of Lent, which include **Palm Sunday**, **Holy Thursday**, **Good Friday**, and **Easter**, are known as **Holy Week**.

Glossary

apartheid—a discriminatory political system in South Africa in which blacks and people of mixed race were segregated from white citizens. Whites also received more rights and privileges than did blacks.

authoritarian—a style of government in which all power is concentrated in one person, or a small group of leaders, and strict obedience to authority is strongly enforced.

commodity—something of use or value, especially an unprocessed material.

consultative—a group that is available to consider facts and provide an opinion or analysis to a decision-making board or assembly.

coup—the sudden, and often violent, overthrow of a government and seizure of political power by a group, such as the military.

diversity—a variety of something, such as lifestyles, ethnic groups, or social practices.

federation—a form of government in which multiple smaller states or regions defer certain powers (such as conducting foreign affairs) to a central government, while retaining some measure of autonomy.

genocide—the deliberate, systematic destruction of a racial, political, or cultural group.

gross domestic product—a measure of the value of all goods and services produced within a country during a one-year period.

inflation—an increase in the supply of money and credit relative to available goods and services, resulting in a continuing rise in the general price level.

infrastructure—the basic facilities and services needed for a community to function, like water, sewer, and power lines, roads, schools, post offices, and prisons.

intervene—to take action or get involved in a situation in order to change something that is happening or prevent an undesirable outcome from occurring.

malaria—an infectious disease common in tropical countries, which is characterized by severe chills and high fevers.

new variant famine—a famine that is not caused by traditional problems such as droughts, floods, or insect infestations. With a new variant famine, traditional ways to resolve the problems caused by the famine are generally useless.

organ—an organization or assembly that acts on behalf of a government.

ratify—to give formal approval to a treaty or agreement so that it becomes valid or operative.

subsistence—providing just enough food to support life.

tuberculosis—an infectious disease that affects the lungs.

Project and Report Ideas

Maps

Draw or print from the Internet a map of Africa with all of its countries identified. Now research each of the five African Economic Communities (AECs): the AMU (Arab Maghreb Union, representing five northern African countries); the ECCAS (Economic Community of Central African States); the COMESA (Common Market of Eastern and Southern Africa); the SADC (Southern African Development Community); and, the ECOWAS (Economic Community of West African States). Find the countries that are members of each AEC and shade each of them according to which AEC they belong to.

Draw or print from the Internet a map of Africa with all of the countries identified. Which countries belong to sub-Saharan Africa? Which do not?

Reports

Write a brief biography of one of the African leaders involved with either the Pan-African congresses, the Organization of African Unity, or the African Union. Some possible choices are Henry Sylvester Williams, W.E.B. DuBois, Timothy Thomas Fortune, Haile Selassie, and Muammar al-Gaddafi.

Write a brief biography of one of Africa's great independence leaders, perhaps using a colorful poster. Possibilities include Leopold Senghor of Senegal, Kwame Nkrumah of Ghana, Julius Nyerere of Tanzania, Jomo Kenyatta of Kenya, or Nelson Mandela of South Africa.

Project and Report Ideas

Research one of the recent or ongoing conflicts or civil wars in Africa (possibilities include the fighting in Sudan, Chad, Somalia, Uganda, Liberia, and Côte d'Ivoire). In a one-page essay, describe which groups are in conflict and why they are fighting. If the conflict has ended, explain how it has been resolved.

Presentations

Imagine that you are a commissioner in charge of one of the African Union Commission's areas of responsibility, such as social affairs or energy. Explain this area to the class. What is the current situation? Should it be improved? What do you think the African Union can or should do to improve it?

Chronology

Before 2.5 million B.C.:	Fossils, rocks, and ancient skeletal remains indicate early humans lived in the Great Rift Valley of East Africa.
Before 200,000:	Evidence suggests that hunter-gatherer communities are established in Africa.
6000–4000:	Societies emerge in areas along the Nile, Niger, and Congo Rivers.
ca. 4500:	Ancient Egyptians develop the first known written language and construct the pyramids.
4000–1000:	Ancient Egypt rises to its peak of power and influence.
ca. 1000–800:	Bantu people migrate from West Africa to southern Africa.
500:	Ancient Nok culture thrives in central Nigeria.
ca. A.D. 120:	The Roman Empire gains control of the North African coast.
4th century:	The Aksum Empire converts to Christianity.
639–641:	Muslim Arab armies conquer Egypt.
700–800:	Islam sweeps across North Africa.
800–1100:	The trans-Sahara gold trade flourishes in the Sahel region.
1000–1400:	Yoruban culture flourishes in West Africa, producing terra-cotta and bronze artwork.
13th century:	The Empire of Mali rises to power.
ca. 1400:	Mali Empire goes into decline; Swahili cities flourish on East African coast.
1441:	The European slave trade begins with a shipment of slaves from West Africa to Portugal.
1480s:	Europeans arrive on the east coast of Africa; the Kongo Kingdom flourishes on the Congo River.
1562:	Britain begins trading slaves from Africa.

1570:	The Portuguese establish a colony in Angola.
1652:	The Dutch establish a colony at the Cape of Good Hope, in southern Africa.
ca. 1717:	The Ashanti Empire rises to power in Ghana.
18th century:	The Atlantic slave trade reaches its height; millions of Africans are shipped to the Americas.
1868:	W.E.B. DuBois, who would become known as the "father of pan-Africanism," is born in Great Barrington, Massachusetts.
1869:	Henry Sylvester Williams born in Arouca, Trinidad.
1885:	European powers mark their spheres of influence in Africa, and establish the borders of their African colonies, at the Berlin Conference.
1893:	The Congress on Africa is held.
1897:	Henry Sylvester Williams founds the Pan-African Association.
1900:	The Pan-African Conference is held.
1911:	Henry Sylvester Williams dies and W.E.B. DuBois takes his place as head of the Pan-African Association.
1912:	The African National Congress (ANC) is founded in South Africa to defend the rights of blacks under white rule.
1919:	The first Pan-African Congress is held; a petition asking for African colonies to be granted the right to rule themselves is sent to Allied leaders at the Paris Peace Conference, but the request is ignored.
1921:	The second Pan-African Congress produces the London Manifesto.
1922:	Egypt becomes a constitutional monarchy, officially independent of Britain.
1923:	The third Pan-African Congress is held.
1927:	The fourth Pan-African Congress is held.
1939:	World War II begins when Nazi Germany invades Poland in September.

Chronology

1941: British Prime Minister Winston Churchill and U.S. President Franklin D. Roosevelt issue the Atlantic Charter. Among its declared principles are the right of all peoples to govern themselves.

1945: World War II ends; a fifth Pan-African Congress is held in Manchester, England.

1954: Gamal Abdel Nasser seizes power in Egypt; British troops are removed from Egypt and Nasser is elected Egypt's first president; Algerian war of independence begins.

1956: Morocco and Tunisia become independent.

1957: Ghana becomes the first of the sub-Saharan African colonies to gain independence.

1958: South Africa officially gains independence from Great Britain.

1960: Seventeen African countries gain independence—Nigeria, Senegal, Mali, Belgian Congo, French Congo, Ivory Coast, Upper Volta (now Burkina Faso), Cameroon, Somalia, Dahomey (now Benin), Mauritania, Madagascar, Niger, Chad, Togo, Gabon, and the Central African Republic.

1962: Algeria wins independence from France after eight years of bloody fighting.

1963: The Organization of African Unity (OAU) is established.

1967–70: Biafran civil war is fought in Nigeria.

1971: Idi Amin assumes power in Uganda, beginning one of the most repressive regimes in Africa.

1974: The fifth Pan-African Congress is held.

1975: Cape Verde, Guinea-Bissau, Mozambique, and Angola gain independence from Portugal.

1980: Rhodesia gains independence and majority rule; changes its name to Zimbabwe.

1989: Civil war breaks out in Liberia, continues through 2003.

1990: Black South African leader Nelson Mandela is released from prison after serving 27 years.

Chronology

1991: The apartheid system is abolished in South Africa and the country prepares for multiracial elections; African Regional Economic Communities are established. These include the Arab Maghreb Union (AMU), the Economic Community of Central African States (ECCAS), the Common Market of Eastern and Southern Africa (COMESA), the Southern African Development Community (SADC), and the Economic Community of West African States (ECOWAS).

1994: At least 800,000 Tutsi civilians are massacred by Hutu vigilantes in Rwanda; Nelson Mandela is inaugurated president of South Africa; the sixth Pan-African Congress is held.

1999: After years of military rule, Nigeria holds democratic elections; Thabo Mbeki replaces Mandela as South Africa's president; Libyan ruler Muammar al-Gaddafi holds the Sirte Conference.

2000: Fighting is halted over the Eritrea-Ethiopian border dispute, though it remains unresolved; the Constitutive Act of the African Union is formally adopted.

2002: The African Union is established.

2003: A new constitution is signed in the Democratic Republic of the Congo and an interim government shares power with rebel leaders.

2004: The African Union sends monitors to Darfur to observe a ceasefire. This force is eventually expanded to some 7,000 peacekeeping troops.

2005: The AU sends a fact-finding mission to Zimbabwe to investigate human-rights violations; the Sudanese government and rebel leaders sign an agreement ending more than two decades of civil war in that country.

2006: Officials from the African Union oversee the signing of a peace agreement in Darfur; the AU considers establishing Pan-African radio and television stations.

2007: The African Union agrees to keep its peacekeepers in Darfur.

Further Reading/Internet Resources

Fowler, Allan. *Africa*. New York: Children's Press, 2001.

Graf, Mike. *Africa*. Mankato, Minn.: Bridgestone Books, 2003.

Kurtz, Jane, ed. *Memories of Sun: Stories of Africa and America*. New York: Amistad, 2003.

Porter, Malcolm and Keith Lye. *Africa*. Austin, Texas: Raintree Steck-Vaughn, 2002.

Rowh, Mark. *W.E.B. Du Bois: Champion of Civil Rights*. Berkeley Heights, NJ: Enslow Publishers, 1999.

Shillington, Kevin. *Causes and Consequences of Independence in Africa*. Austin, Texas: Raintree Steck-Vaughn, 1998.

Internet Resources

http://www.africa-union.org

http://www.ipeacei.org

http://sdrc.lib.uiowa.edu/ceras/locator/igos.html

http://www.bbc.co.uk/worldservice/africa/features/storyofafrica

http://www.live8live.com

http://www.aidsandafrica.com

http://www.duboislc.org/html/DuBoisBio.html

http://www.nepad.org

http://allafrica.com/peaceafrica/organizations

African Union
P.O. Box 3243
Roosevelt Street (Old Airport Area)
W21K19
Addis Ababa
Ethiopia
Tel.: (+251) 1 51 77 00
Fax: (+251) 1 51 78 44
Website: http://www.africa-union.org

Office of the Permanent Observer for the African Union to the United Nations
346 East 50th Street
New York, NY 10022
Tel.: (212) 319-5490
Fax: (212) 319 7135/6509

Africa Action
1634 Eye Street, NW, #810
Washington, DC 20006 USA
Tel.: (202) 546-7961
Fax: (202) 546-1545
Website: africaaction@igc.org

The Ford Foundation Special Initiative for Africa
The Ford Foundation
320 East 43rd Street
New York, NY 10017
Tel.: (212) 573-4952/5067
Email: a.aidoo@fordfound.org

Index

Abacha, Sani, 57
advisory bodies, 44–47
    See also African Union
    (AU)
African Association, 22
    See also African Union
    (AU)
African Central Bank, 47
African Court of Justice
    (judicial system), 40–42
    See also African Union
    (AU)
African Court on Human and
    Peoples' Rights, 41, 52–53
    See also judicial system
    (African Court of
    Justice)
African Investment Bank, 47
African Monetary Fund, 47
African Union (AU)
    advisory bodies, 44–47
    and AIDS, 14, 55–57
    anthem, 43
    and civil conflicts, 14–16,
    29–31, 49–52
    and economies, 14, 47, 55,
    59–62
    and education, 14, 60
    emblem, 41
    European Union (EU) as
    model for, 16–19
    financial institutions,
    46–47

flag, 41
formation of the, 13, *32*, 33
funding for, 62–63
goals of the, 13, 16, 37,
    62–63
and governance, 57–59
and health care, 14, 55–57,
    60
and human rights, 41,
    52–54
judicial system, 40–41
maps, *7*
as the Organization of
    African Unity (OAU),
    28–33
organization of the, 35–47
peacekeeping forces,
    50–51
agriculture, 14, 60
    See also economies
AIDS, 14, 55–57
    See also health care
Angola, 14
anthem, 43
Assembly, 35–36, 38
    See also African Union
    (AU)
Atlantic Charter, 26
AU Commission, 38–39, 53
    See also African Union
    (AU)
Awolowo, Obafemi, 26

Banda, Hastings, 26
Banjul Charter, 41
Berlin Conference, 21–22
Bouteflika, Abdelaziz, 33
Burundi, 50

Cameroon, 60–61
Central African Republic, 51
Chissano, Joaquim, 44, *45*
civil conflicts, 14–16, 29–31,
    49–52
colonialism, European, 21–28
Commission. *See* AU
    Commission
Compaoré, Blaise, *21*
Congress on Africa, 22
Constitutive Act of African
    Union (Sirte Declaration),
    31–33, 35–36, 39–40, *42*,
    44, 58–59
    See also African Union
    (AU)
corruption, government,
    57–59, 61–62
currency, *18*, 19, 46–47

Darfur region, 50–51
    See also civil conflicts
debt, 60–62
    See also economies
"Declaration to the World"
    ("London Manifesto"), 25
Democratic Republic of the

Numbers in ***bold italic*** refer to captions.

Contributors

Professor Robert I. Rotberg is Director of the Program on Intrastate Conflict and Conflict Resolution at the Kennedy School, Harvard University, and President of the World Peace Foundation. He is the author of a number of books and articles on Africa, including *A Political History of Tropical Africa* and *Ending Autocracy, Enabling Democracy: The Tribulations of Southern Africa*.

Russell Roberts is an award-winning writer who has written over two dozen non-fiction books for children on a wide range of topics, including endangered species, Egyptian pharaohs, the Statue of Liberty, Philo T. Farnsworth, Davy Crockett, Alexander Hamilton, Bernardo de Gálvez, colonial American holidays and celebration, Mount Vesuvius and the destruction of Pompeii, and American female medical pioneers. Among the subjects he has written about for adults are baseball, New Jersey history, travel, and memory improvement.

Roberts lives in Bordentown, New Jersey, with his wife, daughter, and an incredibly lazy calico cat named Rusti.